# What's Going On at the TIME Tonight?

story by **GERALD MERCER**

illustrations by **HOLLY DEWOLF**

NIMBUS
PUBLISHING

Nimbus Publishing Limited
3731 Mackintosh St, Halifax, NS  B3K 5A5
(902) 455-4286 nimbus.ca

Printed and bound in China

Cover and interior design: Heather Bryan
Author photo: Margie Costello
Illustrator photo: Reagen DeWolf

Library and Archives Canada Cataloguing in Publication

Mercer, Gerald
What's going on at the time tonight? / Gerald Mercer ;
and illustrator, Holly DeWolf.

Also issued in electronic format.
ISBN 978-1-77108-004-0

1. Children's poetry, Canadian (English).  I. DeWolf, Holly
II. Title.

PS8626.E74W53 2013      jC811'.6      C2012-907398-9

Canada  NOVA SCOTIA Communities, Culture and Heritage  Canada Council for the Arts  Conseil des Arts du Canada

Nimbus Publishing acknowledges the financial support for its publishing activities from the Government of Canada through the Canada Book Fund (CBF) and the Canada Council for the Arts, and from the Province of Nova Scotia through the Department of Communities, Culture and Heritage.

For Benjamin Michael Raymond Weaver, my first grandchild.
May you grow up knowing the Atlantic Ocean
and the treasures that lie within.—G. M.


For Reagen & Hannah—
my two best teachers!—H. D.

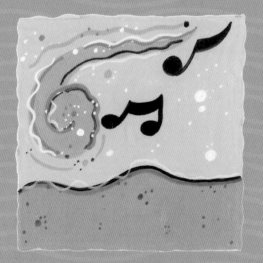

# WHERE will we HOST the TIME tonight?

We could ask if the MUSSELS would share their bed.

We could cozy up tight by the old stage head.

We could gather by the wreckage where the **LOBSTERS** hide.

Then, everything would start at the second high tide.

# WHO will be COMING to the TIME tonight?

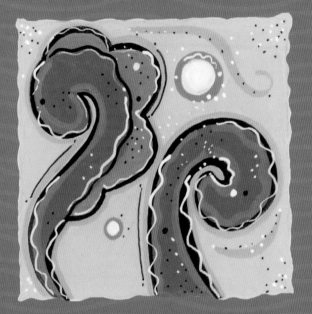

I don't know. Let's make it just right.

The **BARNACLES** are there in great supply.

The **CAPELIN** could choose to swim on by.

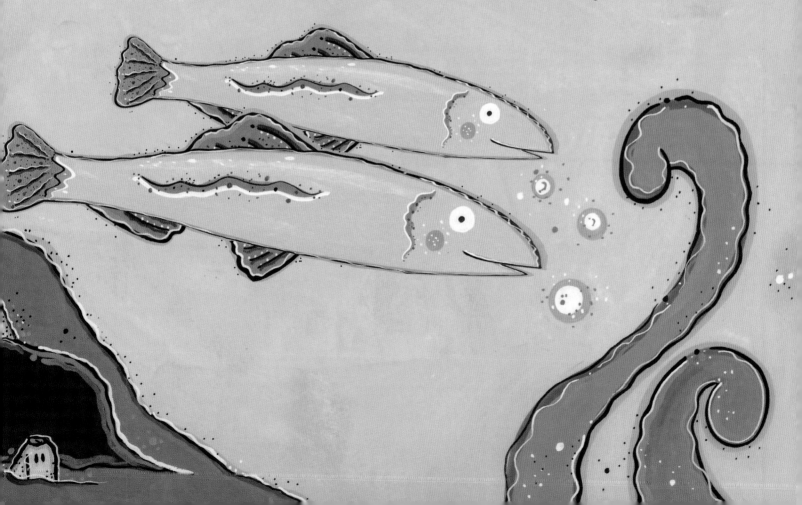

A **CRAB** could sidle and decide to stay.

If a **DOGFISH** comes, we'd keep him at bay.

# WHAT will we DO at the TIME tonight?

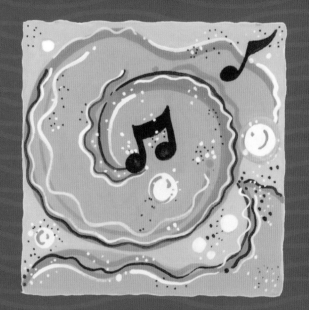

I don't know. Let's make it just right.

We could hire the band,
The **ROCK COD** Pack.

The **SEA LICE** could boogie
on the **FLOUNDER's** back.

The jiggly **JELLYFISH** could ride the wave.

And that inked-up **SQUID**
would have to behave.

# WHAT will we SERVE at the TIME tonight?

I don't know. Let's make it just right.

SEA LETTUCE salad
    dressed with cucumber paste.

Cold KRILL soup
    with some ALGAE to taste.

PLANKTON pot pie and SEAWEED tea.

With creamy KELP cakes, what a feast it'll be!

HOW is it GOING at the TIME tonight?

We KNOW how it's going.

It's going JUST RIGHT!

TRADITIONALLY, people in Newfoundland and Labrador planned parties to while away long evening hours. These parties were called times. People gathered in church basements, community centres, and private homes to share stories, poems, songs, dances, food, and drink. Before the arrival of radio, television, and the internet, times were the main source of entertainment for many Newfoundland and Labrador families. There was nothing that could replace going to a time to listen to recitations, playing or singing songs, having a scuff, and eating a scoff.